Brick or Treat!

By **Matt Huntley** • Illustrated by **Jason May**

Random House 🏠 New York

LEGO, the LEGO logo, the Brick and Knob configurations and the Minifigure
are trademarks and/or copyrights of the LEGO Group.
©2022 The LEGO Group. All rights reserved.
Manufactured under license granted to AMEET Sp. z o.o. by the LEGO Group.

AMEET Sp. z o.o.
Nowe Sady 6, 94-102 Łódź—Poland
ameet@ameet.eu
www.ameet.eu

www.LEGO.com

Published in the United States by Random House Children's Books, a division of Penguin Random House LLC, 1745 Broadway, New York, NY 10019, and in Canada by Penguin Random House Canada Limited, Toronto. Random House and the colophon are registered trademarks of Penguin Random House LLC.
rhcbooks.com
ISBN 978-0-593-38183-0 (trade) — ISBN 978-0-593-48110-3 (ebook)
Printed in the United States of America
10 9 8 7 6 5 4 3 2 1

It was a dark and windy Halloween night. Spooky decorations hung in windows. Jack-o'-lanterns glowed on porches. Costumed trick-or-treaters ran up and down the streets.

"I'm tired of walking," said Matt from inside his penguin costume.

"I think we've visited all the houses," said Kenji, who was wearing an astronaut costume. "Is there anywhere else to go?"

Marina, who was dressed as a cowgirl, said, "Well . . . there is one more house."

At the end of the block, at the top of a hill, there was an old house. It was said that a scientist lived there with his strange creations.

"Isn't that house haunted?" asked Matt.

"Then tonight's the perfect time to go," Marina replied with a smile. She led her friends toward the dark house.

CREAK! The three friends pushed open
the rusty gate and walked across the
overgrown lawn. There were cobwebs in the
windows. A pumpkin glowed by the door.

Marina was about to knock, when the kids
heard a spooky voice: "Come back later!"

The kids were startled. They couldn't see
who was speaking.

Just then, an owl landed on the porch railing. "*Who-o-o* are you? Who invited you? This is the doctor's busiest night. He's in his lab and can't be interrupted by penguins and astronauts."

"Should we come back later?" Kenji asked.
"Maybe we can help," Marina suggested. "The doctor wouldn't be so busy if we helped him."

"The doctor likes to work alone," the owl hooted. "But you should return later for a surprise."

"Yes, a very big surprise," the pumpkin added. Then he and the owl chuckled ominously.

The wind blew and leaves rustled in the tall grass as the children walked away from the house.

"Old houses and talking pumpkins? This is all really strange," Kenji said. "I'm glad we didn't go into the doctor's lab."

"I wonder what the surprise will be," said Marina. "In fact, I want to know what his lab looks like. Let's try to see what Dr. Brickenstein is building."

Marina suddenly ran across the lawn and disappeared into some bushes. Matt and Kenji glanced at each other nervously, then quickly followed.

The friends crept alongside the old house and stopped at a glowing basement window. They crouched and peered in. They could see the doctor's lab!

Machines whirred and clanked. Buttons and bulbs glowed and flickered.

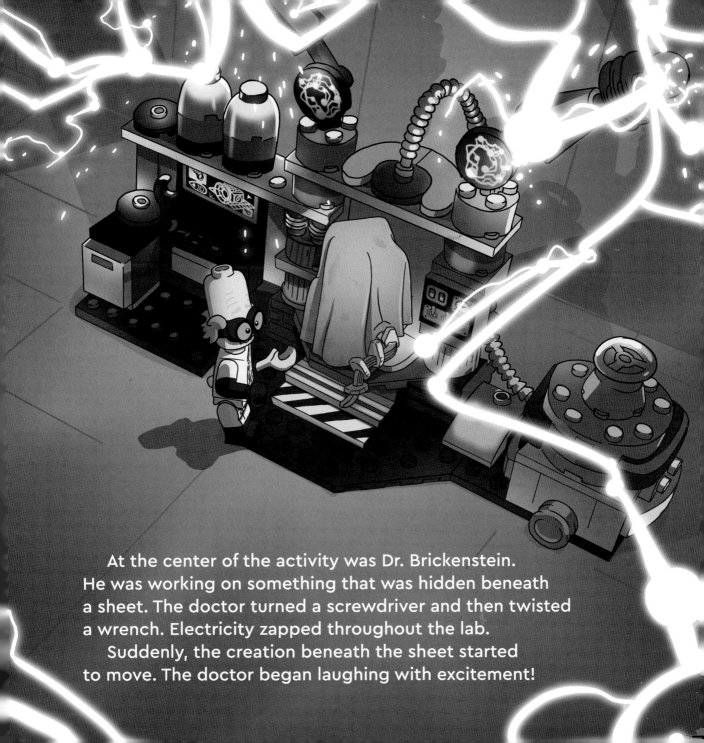

At the center of the activity was Dr. Brickenstein.
He was working on something that was hidden beneath
a sheet. The doctor turned a screwdriver and then twisted
a wrench. Electricity zapped throughout the lab.
   Suddenly, the creation beneath the sheet started
to move. The doctor began laughing with excitement!

Matt, Kenji, and Marina scrambled away from the window.
They scurried through bushes and sprinted across the lawn.
Suddenly, the owl fluttered in front of them.
"Yoo-hoo," he called. "You can't leave now."
The startled friends froze in their tracks.

"That's right," said the pumpkin, rolling along the porch. "You'll miss the surprise."

Just then, the front door creaked open, and Dr. Brickenstein stepped out.

Suddenly, the ground began to shake.

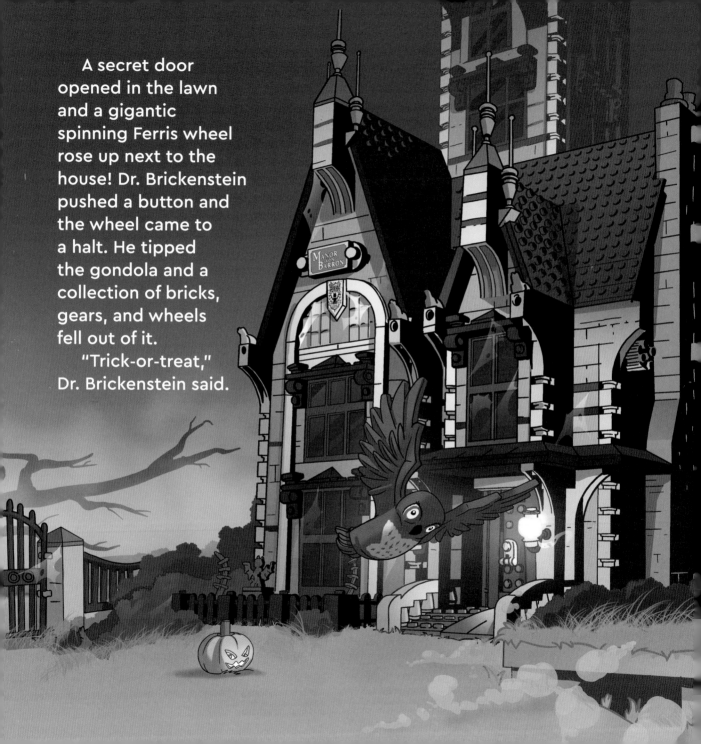

A secret door opened in the lawn and a gigantic spinning Ferris wheel rose up next to the house! Dr. Brickenstein pushed a button and the wheel came to a halt. He tipped the gondola and a collection of bricks, gears, and wheels fell out of it.

"Trick-or-treat," Dr. Brickenstein said.

The three friends studied the pieces and realized they fit together to make . . . a scooter.

"Excellent!" exclaimed Matt. "This is just what I needed. I was getting tired of all this walking and running."

"Or maybe I should say *brick*-or-treat," Dr. Brickenstein said. "You see, I wanted to give you special treats that would let you build things. I think Halloween should be about more than candy. It should be about creativity. It's a night to make costumes and stories—anything you can imagine!"

He pushed another button and the wheel started turning again—and playing carnival music.

All the kids in the neighborhood heard the music and wandered up to the haunted house to see the big wheel. The doctor gave every trick-or-treater a new batch of pieces and parts.

Two girls dressed as ghosts made skateboards.

A boy in a dog costume made a ping-pong table and started playing with a friend who was dressed as a fairy.

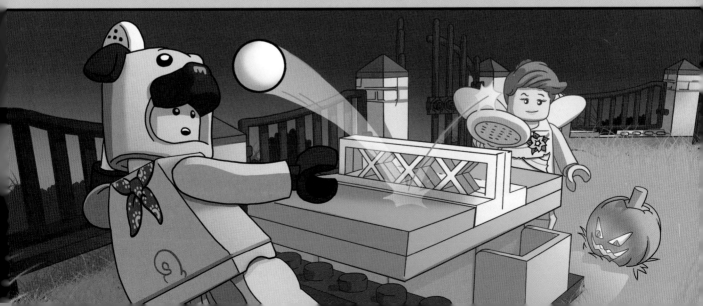

All the kids were laughing and playing in front of Dr. Brickenstein's big old house. Nobody was scared of him anymore. Everyone had a Halloween surprise . . . except for one person, Marina noticed.

"Everyone has a treat except for the doctor," she said.
"Do you think we can make him something?"
Matt and Kenji nodded.

The friends went to work collecting pieces and parts and putting them together behind the bushes. Other trick-or-treaters joined in, adding lights and gears. When they were done, they covered their creation with a sheet and rolled it up to the scientist.

"Dr. Brickenstein," Marina said, "we really like what you've done for us tonight, so we made something for you."

Marina pulled back the sheet and revealed . . . a robot. She turned it on, and it started to walk, making clinking, clanking sounds.

"We thought it could help you in the lab," Matt said, "so we won't have to wait so long to see your incredible creations."

"And maybe the robot could fix up your house a little, so it's not so scary," Matt added.

"That is wonderful!" the doctor exclaimed as the noisy robot waved at him. "Thank you so much! I think I'll call it . . . Clank."

Clank went to the front gate and squirted oil into the hinges. The gate now swung silently. There wasn't a squeak or a creak!

The owl hooted with surprise. "Amazing! But don't fix the house *too* much."

"Yes, please leave it a little creepy," the pumpkin added. "We like things to be Halloweeny around here."

Clank collected some pieces and gears and made itself a lawnmower. Then it went to work cutting the overgrown grass. But Clank didn't trim everything. It snipped a special message into the lawn, and Dr. Brickenstein and all his new friends cheered when they read it: Happy Halloween!